IT LOOKS A LOT LIKE
REINDEER

Study for "Zooson's" family portrait   #3

IT LOOKS A LOT LIKE
REINDEER

by BRIAN P. CLEARY

illustrated by
RICK DUPRÉ

LERNER PUBLICATIONS COMPANY / MINNEAPOLIS

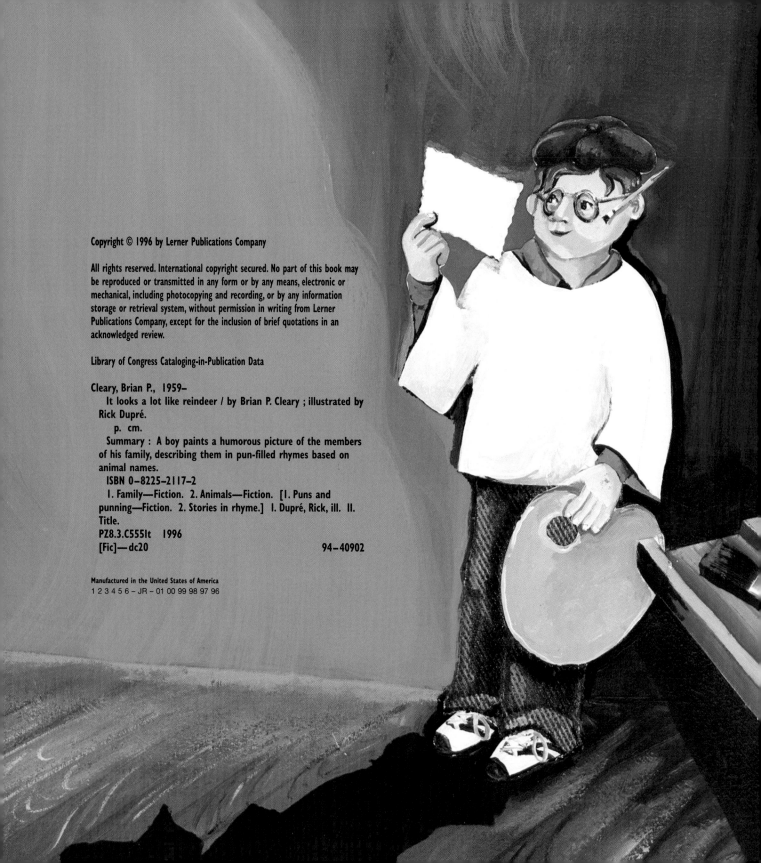

Library of Congress Cataloging-in-Publication Data

Cleary, Brian P., 1959–
    It looks a lot like reindeer / by Brian P. Cleary ; illustrated by Rick Dupré.
        p.   cm.
    Summary : A boy paints a humorous picture of the members of his family, describing them in pun-filled rhymes based on animal names.
    ISBN 0–8225–2117–2
    1. Family—Fiction. 2. Animals—Fiction. [1. Puns and punning—Fiction. 2. Stories in rhyme.] I. Dupré, Rick, ill. II. Title.
PZ8.3.C555lt   1996
[Fic]—dc20   94–40902

Manufactured in the United States of America
1 2 3 4 5 6 – JR – 01 00 99 98 97 96

For Grandma Williams, from whom
most of my silliness flows
B.P.C.

For my sister Barb, who let me
ride on her boyfriend's feet
R.D.

My dad predicts the weather
and he toad my sister once,
"It looks a lot like REINDEER
so be sure to wear your pumps."

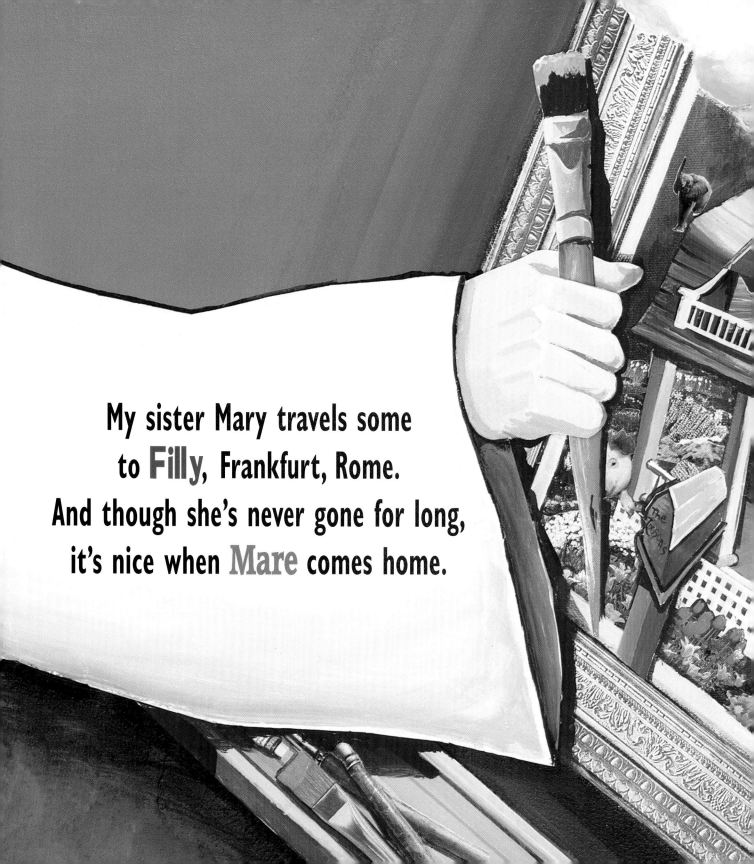

My sister Mary travels some
to **Filly**, Frankfurt, Rome.
And though she's never gone for long,
it's nice when **Mare** comes home.

I *gopher* stays at Grandpa's house—
wolf fish and YAK till dawn.
"My fishing isn't bad," he says,
"but, lord, my **herring's** gone."

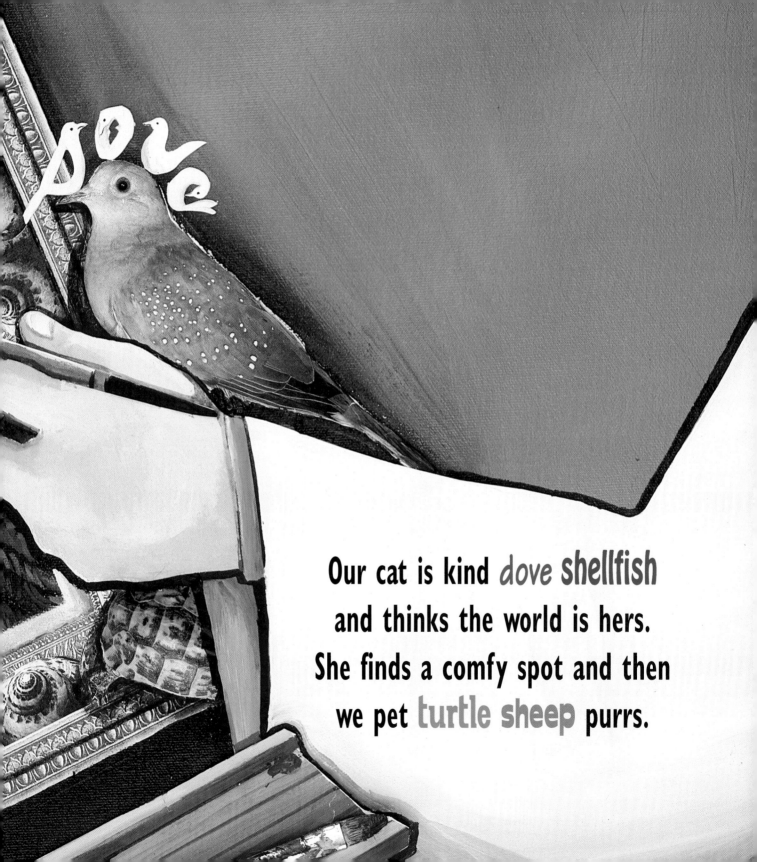

Our cat is kind *dove* shellfish
and thinks the world is hers.
She finds a comfy spot and then
we pet turtle sheep purrs.

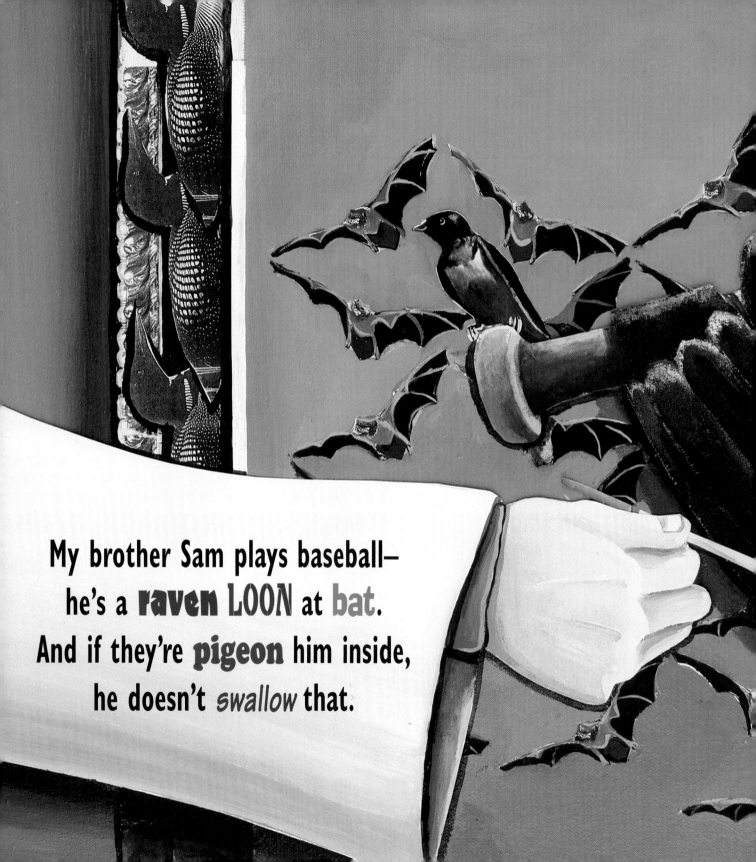

My brother Sam plays baseball—
he's a **raven** LOON at **bat**.
And if they're **pigeon** him inside,
he doesn't *swallow* that.

He'll **fowl** 'em off on **PORPOISE**,
saying, "**TOUCAN** play this game."
And then he'll end up **bunting**—
it's a single just the same.

When **salmon** I go fishing,
we *horse* around and play.
Then *eel* always end up LION
'bout the ones that got away.

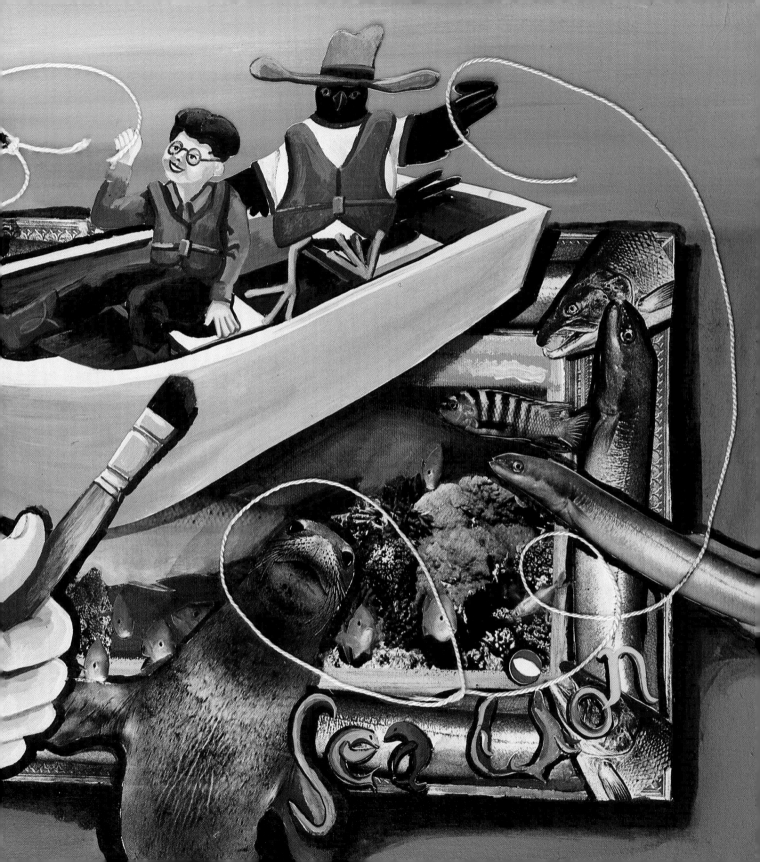

My grandma wears a two-foot wig
that's held on with ape pin.
But if you think her hair is big,
ewe otter sea urchin.

Although she's funny looking,
she's deer as she can be.
When once I asked her for some doe,
she gave a BUCK to me!

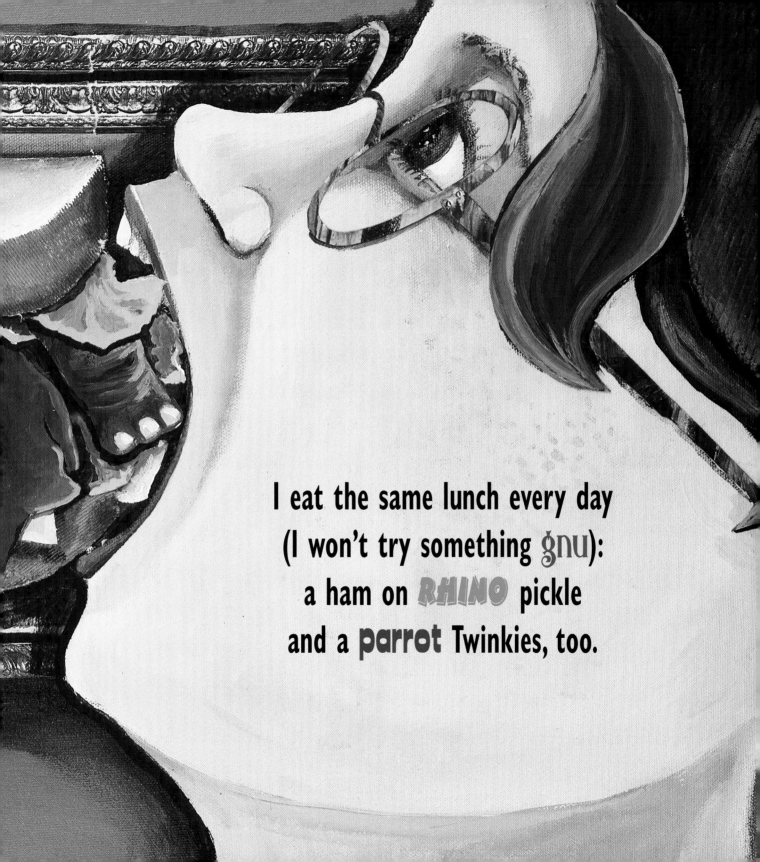

I eat the same lunch every day
(I won't try something gnu):
a ham on RHINO pickle
and a parrot Twinkies, too.

One Saturday my mom asked me
to help **piranha** quest.
She **smelt** a **mouse** inside the house,
but couldn't find the pest.

We searched about the kitchen
from our **perch** atop a chair,
till we discovered what she smelled
was **MOOSE** upon her hare.

When it's stork, I think about
my family, and I roar:
"We could be a lot more normal,
But owl bet we'd be a boar!"

OWL BET

Who would be a **boar**?

1. Toad ....
2. Hare........................
3. Mare.......................
4. Raven Loon................
5. Grandpa Wolf.............
6. Grandma